THE STRANGE
UMBRELLA
AND OTHER STORIES

The Strange Umbrella

and Other Stories

by
ENID BLYTON

Illustrated by
Sally Gregory

AWARD PUBLICATIONS

ISBN 0-86163-408-X

Text copyright © Darrell Waters Limited
Illustrations copyright © 1989 Award Publications Limited

Enid Blyton's signature is a trademark of Darrell Waters Limited

This edition entitled *The Strange Umbrella and Other Stories*
First published 1989
6th impression 1994

Published by Award Publications Limited,
1st Floor, Goodyear House, 52-56 Osnaburgh Street, London NW1 3NS

Printed in Hungary

CONTENTS

The Strange Umbrella

Tiptap the pixie lived in Apple-Tree Cottage in the very middle of Feefo Village. He had two nice little rooms, a kitchen and a bedroom, and outside the cottage was a pocket-handkerchief of a garden – very small, but quite enough for Tiptap to manage.

Now Tiptap was the only pixie in Feefo Village who did no proper work. He had five golden pounds a week of his own, which his old Aunt Tabitha Twinkle sent him, and he just made this do nicely. It bought him bread and butter, cocoa to drink, apple tarts from Mother Buttercup's shop, and fresh eggs from the egg-woman.

Everyone else in the village had their own work to do. The egg-woman looked after her hens and sold their nice brown eggs, the balloon-man sold balloons, Mother Buttercup made lovely cakes and tarts, and the bee-woman got honey from her bees and put it into pots. Everyone did something – except Tiptap, who was the laziest little pixie in the kingdom.

Now one day Tiptap went to see his Aunt Tabitha Twinkle, and she told him she had one or two little jobs for him to do to help her.

'There's my broom that wants mending,' she said. 'The handle has come off.

And there's the garden gate that creaks terribly. You might stop it for me. Oh, and there's my step-ladder too – something's gone wrong with it, Tiptap, and I'd be so glad if you'd see to it.'

'All right,' said Tiptap, rather crossly. He didn't want to mend things for his aunt. He wanted to sit in her nice new hammock and swing himself in the sun.

I'll just have a nice swing first, he thought to himself, and he ran to the hammock. But, do you know, he hadn't been swinging in the sunshine for more than two minutes when he fell fast asleep!

He slept for two hours, and then he heard his aunt calling him in a very cross voice.

'Tiptap! Tiptap! Why haven't you done all I asked you to? There's the gate still creaking, the broom still broken, and the step-ladder not mended! You are a very naughty pixie.'

Tiptap tumbled out of the hammock and ran to the garden shed. He took out the oil-can and ran to the gate to oil it — but he was in such a hurry that he put far too much oil down the hinges, and spilt a lot over the gate itself. He didn't trouble to rub it off with a rag, but left it there and ran to the broken broom.

Quickly he hammered a nail into the handle, and stuck the brush on. Then he looked at the step-ladder. One of the rungs was unsafe, and Tiptap saw that it would need quite an hour's work to take out the bad rung and put in a nice new one.

'Bother!' said the pixie, crossly. 'I can't do that! I shall just stick the old rung in again and tell Aunt Tabitha Twinkle I have mended it. She will never know!'

And that is what the lazy little creature did. Then he ran to his aunt, and said, 'Did you call me, Aunt Tabitha? I have done all the jobs you asked me to, you know, so you really mustn't be so cross.'

'Oh, you're a good little pixie, then,' said his aunt, pleased. 'Come along in and have some pink jelly. It has just set nicely, and I know you're fond of it. Then I'll give you your five pounds and you shall go home.'

Tiptap sat down to eat the jelly. Just as he was finishing it, he saw his aunt's great friend, Mother Smiley-Face, coming in at the gate – and oh my! She had a fine new dress on, and the oil that Tiptap had left on the gate smeared itself all over the blue silk, and *what* a mess it made!

Mother Smiley-Face was very cross. She hurried up to Aunt Tabitha Twinkle and showed her what had happened.

'There's my nice new dress all ruined!' she said. 'Whatever have you been doing to your gate?'

'Oh, that's Tiptap,' said Aunt Tabitha, crossly. 'He didn't wipe the gate clean after oiling it, I suppose!'

'I've come to ask you if you will let me see your new bonnet,' said Mother Smiley-Face, wiping her dress carefully.

'Oh, certainly!' said Aunt Tabitha, pleased. 'I'll fetch it for you. It's on the top of the wardrobe. Get me the step-ladder, Tiptap.'

The pixie fetched the ladder, and his aunt climbed up to get her bonnet – but, oh dear me! When she stepped on the bad rung, it broke, and down she fell, clutching at the parcels on the wardrobe as she did so, so that a whole pile of them fell on the floor in a cloud of dust.

'Oh! Oh! You wicked little pixie! You haven't mended the ladder after all!' said Aunt Tabitha, angrily. 'Oh, I've hurt my knee – and look at all the mess!'

Mother Smiley-Face helped Aunt Tabitha up, and then fetched the

broom to sweep up the mess – but of course the handle flew off as soon as she started sweeping, because Tiptap hadn't mended it properly.

'Well, look at that!' said Aunt Tabitha, now really angry. 'I asked you to do three little things for me, Tiptap, and see how you've done them! I'm ashamed of you! You don't deserve your five pounds a week! In future you shall only have two, and I shan't give you five again until I see that you know how to do a piece of work well.'

So Tiptap was given two pounds instead of five, and sent home in disgrace.

Each week after that only two golden pounds came for him instead of five, and soon Tiptap was in rather a bad way. He could manage to feed himself on two pounds, but if he needed anything new, he had no money to buy it. When his kettle suddenly grew a hole in it, he couldn't buy another. When his spade broke, he had no money for a new one. Of course, he could have mended them if he had set to work with a will, but he was a lazy fellow, and found it much easier to borrow from other folk instead.

So when things went wrong, Tiptap ran round to his friends.

'My clock has stopped and I can't set it going again,' he said to the egg-woman. 'Would you lend me one of yours, please?'

The egg-woman had two clocks, so she lent Tiptap one, thinking that when the pixie had mended his own, he would give hers back. But the lazy fellow didn't bother to try and mend his, now that he had got the egg-woman's.

When his kitchen lamp broke, he ran to Mother Buttercup, who had a spare one, and begged her to lend it to him.

'I'll soon mend mine,' he promised, 'and then you shall have yours back, Mother Buttercup.'

But, of course, *he* didn't trouble to mend his lamp, and poor Mother Buttercup had to go without her second one for weeks and weeks.

Soon Tiptap's cottage was full of things he had borrowed, and his garden shed full of things of his own that he had broken and that were waiting to be mended. But Tiptap didn't mend a single one. No – if people were kind enough to let him have things in their place, well, he would borrow and borrow and borrow!

Now one day he broke his umbrella. He looked at it, and saw that it would take him quite two hours to mend it properly.

'Oh bother!' said Tiptap. 'I'll go and borrow the balloon-man's. I know he has two.'

So he went to the balloon-man, and asked him to lend him his second umbrella, because it was raining very hard and he wanted to go out.

'I'm sorry,' said the balloon-man, 'but I lent my old one to my cousin yesterday, and I've only got my new one left. I can't lend you that, Tiptap, because I've got to go out selling balloons, and I must have an umbrella to keep the rain off me when I sit all day at my corner.'

Then Tiptap went to the bee-woman and asked her to lend him *her* umbrella. But she wouldn't.

'I've only got one, as you know very well, Tiptap,' she said. 'Also, I know that if I lent it to you, you wouldn't bring it back to me. You're getting a very bad name for borrowing, and you'd better stop doing it. Where's that kettle I lent you a month ago?'

Tiptap went red, said good-bye, and ran out. He tried to borrow an umbrella from Gobo the elf who lived in the next cottage, but Gobo had no umbrella at all.

'Now what am I to do?' wondered Tiptap, turning up his coat-collar, because the rain trickled down his neck. 'I do want to go and see Hey-Ho the gnome this morning, and I shall get so wet if I walk across the common without an umbrella!'

But since no one would lend him an umbrella, he had to start off without one. He began to walk over the common, and he felt very cross, for the rain made him wetter and wetter.

Soon he came to Dame Trips' cottage, and he wondered if *she* would lend him an umbrella. So he ran up the garden path and popped his head in at the kitchen window.

'Could you lend me an umbrella?' he asked Dame Trips, who was busy setting out two cups of cocoa on a tray.

'No,' said Dame Trips. 'I haven't one to lend.'

Tiptap ran off again – but just as he passed the front door, what should he see standing outside in the porch but a fine umbrella! Goodness, it *was* a splendid one! It was red with big yellow spots all over it, and the handle was bright green. Instead of a little spike sticking out below the umbrella part, there was a funny knob in the shape of a little face.

'There! Dame Trips said she hadn't an umbrella, and she has, all the time! She told me a story!' said Tiptap. 'I've a good mind to borrow that fine umbrella just to punish her! I can easily leave it here on my way home again.'

He went up to the umbrella. It certainly was a lovely one, the biggest and brightest Tiptap had ever seen. He picked it up and ran down the path with it.

When he was out of sight, he put it up over his head to keep off the rain. Ah, if Tiptap could have seen the little knob of a face at the top then! How it grinned and winked to itself!

Now the way to Hey-Ho's was

towards the west, and Tiptap turned his steps there – but much to his astonishment he found that he couldn't make his legs walk that way! They seemed to want to walk in the opposite direction.

Then he heard a tiny, chuckling laugh, and he wondered where it came from.

It sounds as if it's above the umbrella somewhere, he thought, so he peeped over the edge of it and looked – and he saw that little grinning knob of a face, winking and blinking at him for all it was worth!

'Ooh!' said Tiptap, in a fright. 'Ooh! This umbrella's magic! I must throw it away at once, before it does me any harm!'

He tried to fling it from him, but dear

me, he couldn't let go of the handle! It seemed to hold on to his hand! Tiptap tried to take his hand away, but he couldn't. The handle closed round his fingers and held him fast.

'Ooh!' said Tiptap, beginning to cry. 'It *is* magic! *Now* what's going to happen!'

He hadn't long to wait before he knew, for the umbrella suddenly began to blow along towards the north-east, just as if a great wind was behind it. It pulled Tiptap along after it, and the poor little pixie found himself running fast over the common, unable to do anything else. The big red umbrella pulled him along at a tremendous pace, and Tiptap was soon out of breath – but he *couldn't* let go of the handle.

'Where's it taking me to?' he wondered, the tears pouring down his cheeks in fright. 'Oh dear! It can't have belonged to Dame Trips after all. It must have belonged to someone who was visiting her! Oh, why did I take it?'

At last, after taking Tiptap about

five miles over hill and dale, the umbrella came to a little white house set on a hillside. On the gate was a name – Wizard Ho-Hum's Cottage.

Then Tiptap was more afraid than ever. He knew that the wizard would be very angry to find his umbrella had been taken from Dame Trips, for he would have to walk home in the rain.

The umbrella took Tiptap to the front door, and there it stayed. There didn't seem to be anyone in the house at all. Wizard Ho-Hum was out. He had gone to see his sister, Dame Trips – and my goodness, when he came out and found that someone had taken his umbrella, what a rage he was in.

'Well, I shall find the thief outside my front door, waiting for me!' he said to himself. 'My umbrella will be sure to take him there! But just look at this rain! How wet I shall get!'

So he did, for the rain poured down as he went across the common. When he at last got home, he was in a fine temper. He saw the umbrella by his front door, the handle still holding fast to Tiptap's hand, and the little head at the top chuckling and laughing for all it was worth.

'Ho!' he shouted, frowning angrily at Tiptap. 'So *you're* the thief, are you?'

'Please, no,' said Tiptap, in a small voice. 'I thought it was Dame Trips' umbrella, and I just borrowed it.'

'*I've* heard all about you!' said the wizard. 'You're the nasty, horrid little fellow that breaks your own things and goes about borrowing other people's and never takes them back again! Well, *I* call that stealing! Yes, I do! I'll teach you to steal *my* umbrella!'

He opened his front door, took the

umbrella away from Tiptap's hand, and closed it. Then he stood it in a corner, and ordered Tiptap to go in.

'Now, I want a handy-man,' he said to the frightened pixie. 'You can choose what you will do – either I take you to Pop-Off the policeman, and tell him you stole my umbrella, or *you* can be my handy-man for six weeks, and do all my odd jobs till my other man comes back. If you try to run away, the red umbrella will come after you and catch you. Now, which will you choose?'

'P-p-p-please, I'll b-b-b-be your handy-m-m-m-man!' stammered the pixie, who couldn't bear the idea of being taken to Pop-Off.

'Then make yourself useful straight

away!' commanded Ho-Hum. 'Take a pail and clean all the windows. Then peel some potatoes and prepare dinner for me.'

Tiptap set to work. How he made those windows shine! Then he peeled the potatoes, and put a milk pudding into the oven. After that the wizard made him chop wood till his arms ached.

What a time the pixie had for the next few weeks! He was up at day-break, and he wasn't allowed to go to bed till he had finished every single job there was to be done. He had to keep the cottage clean and tidy, cook all the meals, work in the garden, chop the wood and mend anything that got broken, for the wizard wouldn't hear of buying or borrowing fresh things.

Once Tiptap made up his mind to run away, and in the night he crept out of the cottage – but he hadn't gone very far before he heard a little chuckle behind him, and, oh my! In the moon-light what should he see but that red umbrella just behind him! It opened itself all of a sudden and the handle caught hold of Tiptap's hand. Then he was dragged all the way back to Ho-Hum's.

The wizard found him outside the front door in the morning, held tightly by the umbrella.

'Ho, so you thought you'd try to run away, did you?' he said. 'Well, you shall be spanked for that!'

So Tiptap got a spanking, and his day's work was twice as hard as before.

When he had been at Ho-Hum's for a month, he found that he began to like his work. It was fun to make the cottage shine like a new pin. It was lovely to dig in the garden in the sun. It was exciting to mend something that was broken and make it as good as new again. Really, Tiptap quite enjoyed himself, and he began to sing and whistle at his work like a blackbird in spring.

'Ah, you're beginning to see that it is a fine thing to work!' said Ho-Hum one morning. 'What a nasty, lazy, good-for-nothing fellow you used to be, to be sure! See how clever your hands are, when you set them to something. Why, I shall be quite sorry to lose you tomorrow, when my old handy-man comes back.'

'Is he coming back tomorrow?' asked Tiptap in dismay. 'Oh! I *shall* be sorry to go! It *will* seem funny going back home with nothing to do.'

'Well, since you're such a good hand at mending and making,' said

Ho-Hum, 'why don't you make yourself the handy-man of Feefo Village? I hear there isn't one there, and I'm sure folk would be very glad of one.'

'That's a splendid idea!' said Tiptap, pleased. 'Hurrah! I'll soon show everyone I'm not lazy or good-for-nothing!'

The next day Ho-Hum's old handy-man came back, and Tiptap said goodbye to the wizard, who gave him a little tie-pin in the shape of a red umbrella, to remind him never to be lazy again. Tiptap stuck it proudly into his tie and marched home.

As soon as he got to Apple-Tree Cottage, and had set it in order again, he went to his garden shed, there were all the dozens of things he had broken and put there weeks before. He set to work to mend them, and by the end of the week there were all his tools, pots and pans, and everything else as good as new. Then Tiptap took back all the things he had borrowed, thanked the people who had kindly lent them to him, and said he was sorry he had kept them so long.

'I'm going to set up as handy-man to the village,' he told everyone. 'Let me have anything broken or spoilt, and I'll mend it for you for a penny or two. I want to do something for my living now!'

How astonished and pleased all the people were! They let Tiptap have all their broken things and he mended them splendidly. Soon he had quite a lot of money in his purse, and wasn't he proud of it!

Then one day his Aunt Tabitha came

to see him, to give him all the pounds he hadn't had whilst he had been away.

'You shall have five pounds a week again now!' she said, when she found out how hard Tiptap was working, and how changed he was. But Tiptap wouldn't take a penny!

'No, thank you, Aunt Tabitha Twinkle,' he said. 'I've found out that it is a hundred times nicer to earn money myself than to take it from someone else for doing nothing. Please keep it yourself, or give it to the Hospital for Sick Brownies. In future I'm going to work hard and be happy.'

He kept his word, and his Aunt Tabitha Twinkle sent the money to the Brownie Hospital, which was very much delighted to have it. As for Tiptap, you should hear him whistle and sing as he mends pots and pans and sharpens knives. It really is lovely to listen to him. He still has his tie-pin, and he wouldn't part with it for the world!

'That was the best thing that ever happened to me!' he often says. 'I'll never be sorry that strange umbrella took me away!'

The Enchanted Mirror

Did you ever hear about the enchanted mirror? Well, it was a most extraordinary thing, brought one day by the school inspector! He set it up in the classroom and smiled round at the children.

'I wonder if you all know what you are like?' he said. 'I expect you each think yourselves very fine and hardworking, perhaps very clever, good-tempered and lovable? Well, you may be, for all I know! Perhaps you'd like to see yourselves in my enchanted mirror?'

'Oh, yes, please, sir!' shouted the children eagerly. The inspector set the mirror up against Miss Brown's desk.

It was a big one. The children jiggled about excitedly. The inspector beckoned to fat little Johnny. Out he came, his plump face red with excitement. He looked into the mirror.

Do you know what he saw there? He saw a nice little fat piggy-wig, dressed in coat and knickerbockers! What a shock he got! 'I'm afraid you must be a bit greedy, little piggy!' whispered the inspector in his ear. He beckoned to Lucy, a timid, shy little girl. She came out and looked into the mirror, too.

Goodness! She saw a little rabbit there, dressed in her blue frock, with big, startled eyes and a woffly nose. 'I think you must be too afraid of things!' said the inspector kindly. 'You must stand up for yourself, you know!'

Jack came out next – a nice little boy who never tried to use his brains, but was quite content to be at the bottom of everything, although he needn't have been. Oh dear! What did *he* see in that mirror? A little grey donkey with big ears, its head sticking out of Jack's red jersey! 'You *needn't* be such a little donkey, you know!' whispered the inspector. 'You've got plenty of brains, really!'

Betty came out – spiteful little Betty, always ready to say a mean thing, or give a sly pinch. She didn't like what *she* saw in the mirror! She saw a snarling, spitting little kitten, with claws outstretched. She went red.

'Keep your claws in, Betty!' said the inspector. 'Don't be catty!'

Then came Rita, always dependable, honest and trustworthy. She looked shyly into the strange mirror. She saw her own self there, more beautiful than she had ever imagined, for she was not a pretty child. The inspector nodded his head, pleased. 'Stay as you are,' he said. 'Do not change yourself, Rita.'

Poor Benny came next – a mean little

boy, cowardly, and yet always on the watch to hit someone smaller than himself. The inspector was sad to see a mean little rat looking out at him from the mirror. 'Dreadful, isn't it, Benny?' he said. And Benny nodded, shocked and horrified. Was he really like that? He would hurry up and change his ways, then!

Molly saw a nice fluffy goose. And how often had Miss Brown told her that? How often had she said, 'Molly, you really are a goose? You'll grow feathers one day!' And now, sure enough, there she was in the mirror, feathers and all!

There isn't time to tell you of sturdy, fearless Harry, who saw a lion in the mirror! Nor of chatterbox Jenny with the screeching laugh, who saw a parrot, or fussy Tracey, who saw a hen, or trustworthy David, who saw a big faithful dog. And, of course, what you really want to know is – what would *you* see if you looked into the school inspector's enchanted mirror!

Sly-One's Ice-Cream

Sly-One the gnome was walking down the road that leads to our land. Just in front of him was Crinkle the wise man. Sly-One kept well behind him, for he was rather afraid of Crinkle.

Suddenly something rolled out of Crinkle's long cloak, and slid to the grass at the side of the lane. It was a shining golden pound! When Sly-One came up to it, he picked it up quickly and slipped it into his pocket.

Crinkle didn't know he had dropped anything, and went walking slowly on. Sly-One knew quite well that he ought to have run up to him and given him his pound – but he was a mean fellow, and wanted to keep it for himself. He deserved a hard spanking for his dishonesty, but Crinkle didn't even guess what had happened.

Sly-One walked into our land – and the first thing he saw was an ice-cream man selling lovely cold ice-creams. Now Sly-One had never seen an ice-cream before, and he wondered what

they were. He went up to the children who were standing round the van and looked at what they were eating.

'What does it taste like?' he asked.

'Ooh, don't you know?' said the boy he was speaking to. 'Here, have a bite of mine!'

Sly-One took a bite. Oh, what a delicious taste! Oh, what a glorious feeling as the ice-cream slipped down his throat, cold and sweet!

'How much are they? A pound?' he asked the boy.

'No, these are only fifty pence,' said the boy. 'For a pound you can have a great big one in a cardboard box to take home with you.'

So Sly-One paid a pound, and the man handed him a cardboard box with the yellow ice-cream inside. The gnome was delighted.

I'll take it home and have it for my tea, he thought. And I'll eat it all myself, every bit. I shan't ask anyone to share it!

He ran off with the ice-cream. The

day was very, very hot, and the sun shone down warmly. The road seemed to burn Sly-One's feet as he went along, and he longed to be home in his cool parlour.

Now, as he went on his long way home, the sun shone straight on to the thin cardboard box that held the ice-cream. It began to melt. It turned into a cold yellow liquid that began to drip out of the corners of the box. At first Sly-One didn't notice this, but when he saw it, he was astonished.

'Now what's happened?' he wondered, for he had no idea that ice-cream melted. He undid one end of the box and looked for his ice-cream. But it wasn't there! Instead there was something that looked like thin yellow custard, and this is what was dripping steadily out of the box.

'Oh!' cried Sly-One in disgust. 'What's happened? Where's my ice-cream? That nasty, horrid cheat of an ice-cream man has given me this yellow mess, instead of a beautiful ice-cream! Oh, to think of that! Well, I can't eat it! I shall throw it away!'

And with that Sly-One flung the box of melted ice-cream through the air. Just at that very moment someone came round the corner, and the ice-cream hit him on the head, bursting its box, and splashing him all over with yellow cream.

Who should it be but Crinkle the wise man! How angry he was! He cleaned the ice-cream from his face, and glared at Sly-One.

'Oho!' he said to the frightened gnome. 'So it's you, is it? What do you mean by this, I should like to know? There's no doubt that you need a good spanking!'

So Sly-One got his spanking after all, which served him right. Crinkle's hand was very hard, and soon Sly-One was running howling down the street.

'I'll never steal a pound again!' he wept. 'I never, never will!'

And he never, never did!

Stones for a Horse

Tom was very cross. His father had told him to fetch Bess, the old horse, from the field on the hill and take her to Farmer Brown's, who wanted to borrow her for a day's work.

'It's Saturday,' he grumbled. 'I've been at school all the week, Dad – can't I have a day off for once? I told Billy Jones we'd take our lunch and walk over to the next village to see the football match.'

'You'll do as you're told, my boy, without any fuss!' said his father sternly. 'If you go now, and bring Bess back at once, you will have plenty of time to call for Billy and walk over to the match.'

It was a cold day and the roads were like ice. Tom sulkily put on his thick coat and started off. Bother Bess!

He walked down the slippery hill, and then cut across the fields up the opposite hill towards the big field where Bess stood, waiting to be fetched to work. She was a big and gentle old horse, but she was not very fond of Tom, who was a rough and impatient little boy.

'Come on, now!' shouted Tom, holding open the gate for Bess. 'Hurry yourself! You're going to Farmer Brown's!'

Bess understood. She lumbered out of the gate at a canter, and Tom gave her a cut with his switch as she passed. Down the fields she went, keeping well in front of Tom and his switch, and then turned into the lane to go up the hill to the farm.

But that hill was like an ice-slide! Bess dug her hoofs into the road, but

she found herself slipping all over the place. She found it very difficult to prevent herself from falling down.

Tom was angry. 'Get on there, get on!' he shouted from some distance behind. But Bess couldn't get on, no matter how she tried. Then Tom lost his temper. He picked up a handful of stones and threw them at Bess. They clattered all round her and frightened her terribly. She struggled again and nearly fell over. She could *not* get up that icy hill. Tom was in a real rage now and threw more and more stones at the horse. He was afraid that he would be too late to go to the football match.

Then someone shouted to him: 'Hey, what do you think you're doing with those stones?' Tom turned. It was Billy Jones, who had come to look for him to go to the match.

'Can't you see!' yelled Tom. 'I'm throwing them at this silly horse to make her go up the hill.'

'That's the wrong way to use stones,' said Billy at once. 'Look here!'

He ran to the edge of the lane and picked up handfuls of pebbles. Then he went over to the struggling horse and spoke gently to her, and scattered pebbles under her feet. Back he went and got more stones. Soon Bess was able to tread the road safely, for the stones helped her to grip the road.

'Use stones if you like, but not for *throwing*!' said Billy. Tom didn't say anything, but I expect he felt ashamed of himself, don't you?

Ripple gets a Necklace

Ripple was a water-pixie. She lived in the Long Pond where the water-lilies grew, and she was as pretty as a picture and as proud as a peacock. She swam in the pond all day long, talked to the big frogs, tickled the old fish, and teased the moorhens that came to nest there.

'You know, Ripple would be so nice if she wasn't so conceited!' said the water-vole one day, as he sat nibbling a water-plant. 'She's always showing off!'

'She cuts the water-lily leaves to pieces, trying to make herself new dresses every week!' said the moorhen, pecking a bit of the vole's plant. 'Do you think it is safe to nest here this spring,

water-vole? Last year Ripple kept tipping my babies out of their nest whenever I swam off. It didn't really matter, because they could swim as soon as they were hatched – but it made them so tired having to climb back a score of times a day!

'Oh, Ripple doesn't care how she teases anyone!' said the vole. 'She tied a water-beetle and a dragonfly grub together the other day, and they were so angry that they nearly ate each other! She's so vain that she thinks she can do anything!'

Now the next day Bufo, the large old toad who lived under a big stone on the bank of the pond, gave invitations to everyone in the pond. They were to come to a party at his end of the pond, and have games and fun. Ripple was to go, too – and she at once began to think

what kind of dress she could make for herself.

'I shall be the prettiest person there!' she said. 'All the others are ugly! I'll have a new dress, and a new ribbon in my hair, and a new necklace!'

Well, she cut up five lily leaves for a dress. The lilies were angry, for the leaves were new and a very pretty red colour underneath. But Ripple didn't care!

She asked the water-weed for a ribbon, and she tied it in her waving hair. Now for a necklace!

'I'll get some water-snail shells and thread them together!' she said.

'Oh no, you won't!' said the snails, and they went to hide.

And then Ripple found some lovely long strands of white jelly-like stuff, set with little black beads, threaded in and out of the water-plants. It was toad-spawn, but she didn't know it! 'Just right for a necklace!' she cried. She unwound it carefully, and then wound it round her own neck. There was enough to make six rows of black and white beads!

Ripple was delighted and very proud. She couldn't think why everyone laughed when they saw her! The party day was the next day, very bright and warm and sunny. Ripple went along with everyone else to old Bufo, the toad. He frowned when he saw her and seemed very cross. But Ripple didn't care. She knew she looked beautiful in her new dress and necklace.

And then she felt something tickling her. Something wriggled down her front, and something wriggled down her back! She screamed.

'What is it? There's something crawling all over me!'

And indeed there was – for the toad-spawn necklace had hatched into tadpoles that had wriggled down her neck! There were dozens of them, little black things that tickled all the time!

'It serves you right,' said Bufo, looking as black as thunder. 'How *dare* you come to my party wearing a necklace of my eggs? Go home at once!'

Ripple didn't go home. She ran right away from that pond, for she was so ashamed of herself. So the moorhen has built her nest there once again, for now she knows that her nestlings will be safe!

The Great Big Bumble-Bee

One morning Louise was playing with her dolls in the nursery when her mother came in.

'What are you playing at, darling?' she asked.

'I'm playing at having a wedding with my dolls,' said Louise. 'But I haven't any white frock nice enough to dress Angelina in, Mummy. She's the bride, you know.'

'Well, if you run upstairs to the attic, and look in the big black trunk near the window, you'll find an old white frock of mine,' said Mother. 'Bring it down, and I'll help you to cut it up and make a lovely wedding-dress for Angelina.'

So Louise ran upstairs to the attic,

and went to the black trunk. She lifted up the lid and looked inside. There, wrapped in tissue paper, was an old white satin dress of Mother's. Just as Louise was going to lift it out, she heard a loud buzzing noise, and looked round to see what it was.

'Goodness, it's a big bumble-bee!' she said. 'I've never seen such a big one before! Poor thing, it's got into the attic, and now it can't find the way out.'

The great bee was buzzing up and down the window-pane, and Louise went to look at him. His body was covered with brown and yellow fur, and his wings whirred so quickly that they made the loudest buzzing Louise had ever heard.

'Look! Get out of the space at the top of the window,' said Louise. 'That's where you flew in, bumble-bee.'

But the bee didn't understand. It flew up and down the glass, up and down, frightened and unhappy. It wanted to get out into the garden, where there was sunshine and plenty

The Great Big Bumble-Bee

of flowers, and it *couldn't* find the way.

Louise felt sorry for it. She did not like to touch it, for she was much too afraid that it would sting her – but she couldn't leave it there in the attic, buzzing up and down the window all day long.

What can I do for the poor thing? thought Louise. Perhaps if I got a piece of paper and put it under the bee and then guided it up to the top of the window, it would have the sense to fly out.'

She fetched a piece of paper, and then put it gently below the bumble-bee. Her hand trembled, for she really was afraid it might sting her, but she didn't draw back, even when the bee buzzed more loudly than ever.

She pushed it carefully right to the top of the window – then BUZZ! The bee flew right out into the garden, and Louise could hear it no longer. It had gone back to the flowers.

Then the little girl went to the black trunk and took out the white satin dress she had come to fetch. She carried it downstairs, and soon she and her mother were busy cutting out a lovely wedding-dress for Angelina.

It *was* a beauty! They worked hard at it all day long, and then dressed the doll in her new frock after tea. She looked simply lovely.

'Oh, Mummy, could I take Angelina in her wedding-dress with me, when I go out to tea at Auntie Mary's tomorrow?' asked Louise.

'Yes,' said Mother. 'I'm sure Auntie Mary would like to see her.'

So next day, when it was time to start out for her auntie's house, and Louise was washed and dressed in her blue cotton dress, she picked up Angelina, and carried her with her.

'It's a good thing it has stopped raining,' said Mother, 'or Angelina might have got wet. The sun is shining now, so you will be all right. Don't tread in the puddles, darling!'

Off went Louise, carrying Angelina in her lovely new wedding-dress. She *was* glad the rain had stopped.

Just as Louise had gone halfway to her Auntie Mary's house, a big dog came running up, splashing through all the puddles. He ran straight to Louise, and sniffed at her legs.

'Go away,' said Louise, holding Angelina out of his reach. 'You're treading on my shoes with your muddy paws. Go away!'

Suddenly the dog jumped up at the doll, and tried to snatch it from Louise. His muddy paws left a dirty mark on the doll's new dress, and Louise was very upset.

'Oh, *do* go away!' she said to the dog. 'Stop jumping up at Angelina.'

But the dog wouldn't stop. He thought Louise was having a game with him, and he meant to get Angelina and chew her up. Louise was in despair. Whatever could she do to make him stop? There was nobody near by at all who could help. The dog jumped higher, and Louise felt certain that he would soon get her doll.

Then suddenly there came a loud buzzing sound – and down flew a great big furry bumble-bee! He flew straight at the naughty dog, and sat on his nose.

'Wuff!' went the dog in fright, for the bee stung him hard.

The bee flew off his nose, circled round Louise's head once or twice and then flew off again. The dog rubbed his nose with his paw, and then, whining loudly, ran off home down the road.

'Oh, fancy that bee helping me like that!' said Louise. 'Why, it must have been the same one that *I* helped yesterday! It looked just as big and beautiful, and it had just as loud a buzz. Oh, I *am* glad I helped it to fly out of the attic window. If I hadn't, it might still be there now, and wouldn't have been able to save Angelina today!'

Off she went to her auntie's, and told her all about her adventure with the dog and the bee.

'That kind big bumble-bee saved Angelina from being chewed to pieces,' said Louise. 'I'm *sure* it was the same bee that I helped out of the window, don't you think so, Auntie?'

I think it must have been, too – don't you?

The Little Clockwinder

Dickory Dock was the clockwinder to the king of Elfland. The king was very fond of clocks and he had a great many. He liked them all to show the same time, and to strike and chime exactly at the right minute. Dickory Dock was supposed to wind them each night – but, you know, he often didn't, and then the clocks went wrong.

One day the king gave him a little magic key. 'Look, Dickory Dock,' he said, 'here is an enchanted key that will wind up anything in the world, no matter what it is – but you, of course, must simply use it for clocks. Instead of keeping a hundred different keys, as you have always had to do, you may now throw them all away and use just this one for every clock in the palace.'

Dickory Dock was delighted – but, even though his work was now much easier, he didn't always remember to wind up the clocks. And one day the king was so cross that he spanked Dickory Dock hard with one of his best red slippers.

Then wasn't Dickory Dock in a temper! How he vowed he would punish the king for spanking him! What a lot of rubbish he talked – and in the end, he thought of the naughtiest, silliest idea imaginable.

'I'll use my magic key and wind up everything in the palace!' he cried. Straight away he began to do this. He wound up every chair, big and small, every table, round or square, every stool and every bookcase. He even wound up the books, the vases and the cushions – and when the king and queen came home that night, what a strange and mysterious sight met their eyes!

'Bless us all!' cried the queen, as a table came dancing up to her. 'What's this!'

'Mercy on us!' shouted the king, as two chairs ran up to him and danced round him. 'What's happened!'

'Look at that stool!' cried the queen. 'It's dancing with my best red cushion! Everything's alive!'

'Dickory Dock has been using the magic key I gave him!' stormed the king in a rage. 'Get away, you clumsy great table, you're treading on my toe. Just look at those books rushing round the room! Where's Dickory Dock? Fetch him at once!'

Dickory Dock was hiding behind the door.

A footman peeped into the room when he heard the king shouting, and in a second he caught the mischievous clockwinder by the shoulder, and brought him before the king. Two or three cups came and ran round them, and a saucer rolled all the way up the stately footman's leg. It was really most peculiar.

'Go away from Elfland at once!' roared the king in a fury. 'Never come back! Give me your key, and I'll wind you up so you'll have to keep on walking and never stop. That will be a good punishment for you!'

With that he dug the magic key into the frightened elf and wound him up. Poor Dickory Dock! He started running off and it wasn't long before he came to our land. He has been here ever since. What do you suppose he does? He winds up the dandelion clocks, of course! He's just as careless over those as he used to be over the clocks in the palace, and that is why they are so seldom right! Puff one and see!

It's Going to Rain!

Old Dame Twinkle didn't know *what* to do with her dreamy husband. He did do such silly things. He never thought about what he was doing, and so he used to brush his hair with his toothbrush, clean his boots with the grate-polish and look for hens' eggs in the dog-kennel. So you can guess what a bother he was to look after.

The thing that worried Dame Twinkle most of all was the habit Mr Twinkle had of going out for a walk, carrying his umbrella and mackintosh – and then, if it rained, he came back *still* carrying his umbrella and mackintosh! And, of course, he was wet through!

'Twinkle, why *don't* you put on your mackintosh and put up your umbrella when it rains?' Dame Twinkle would cry in despair. 'What *is* the sense of taking them if you don't use them? Can't you *see* when it is going to rain, and *feel* when it is pouring down?'

'I don't walk with my eyes on the sky all the time,' said Mr Twinkle. 'A-*tish*-oo!'

'There! You've got *another* cold,' said Dame Twinkle. 'Off to bed with you!'

Well, you can imagine that Dame Twinkle was very worried about her husband always catching colds because he got wet through so often. And at last she went to Witch Green-Eyes to ask her for a spell to stop Mr Twinkle from being so foolish.

'I can't give you a spell for that,' said Witch Green-Eyes. 'It is the hardest thing in the world to stop a stupid person from being foolish. It can't be done.'

'Well, what can I do, then?' said poor Dame Twinkle. 'There he goes, out for his walk, his eyes on the ground all the time! He never thinks of looking up to see what the weather is like!'

'If he looks at the ground all the time, why not put something there to warn him!' said the witch. 'Leave it to me, Dame Twinkle. I will think of something.'

So she thought hard; and then she went down the lanes and through the fields where Mr Twinkle loved to walk, carrying a pot of bright scarlet paint. With it she painted the petals of a small white flower that grew by the wayside, and into the flower she put a rain-spell so that it would close up its petals tightly whenever rain was near.

Then she called on Dame Twinkle. 'Tell your husband to watch the bright scarlet flower by the wayside,' she said. 'Red for danger, you know! When it closes its petals, rain is coming – so Mr Twinkle will be warned and will put on his mackintosh in time!'

And now Mr Twinkle has no more colds, because the little flower always warns him when rain is near. Do you know what its name is? It is the scarlet pimpernel, and it still has some of the old magic in it – for, as you will see, it closes its red petals tightly whenever rain is near!

The Magic Silver Thread

Once upon a time there lived a wizard called Deep-Eyes, who had one son called Ho-Ho, a baby boy who was twelve months old. Ho-Ho used to crawl about the wizard's work-room whilst Deep-Eyes was making his spells, and one day a dreadful thing happened.

Deep-Eyes was making a spell for a witch who wanted her apple trees to grow bigger and stronger. He mixed all kinds of things together, and put the mixture in a blue bowl to cool. He set it on a low table, and then took down one of his magic books to read.

The baby found the bowl and liked the look of the golden, shining water inside. He suddenly took hold of it, jerked it into the air, and spilt it all over himself! Then what a to-do there was!

Ho-Ho cried and licked the mixture that was running all down his face. It soaked his clothes, and made him shiver. The wizard shouted aloud in dismay and ran to his little son. The mother came rushing into the room, and picked him up.

'What a silly you are to stand bowls of water about!' she said to her husband, the wizard.

'It wasn't a bowl of water,' said the wizard, with a groan. 'It was a golden spell I had made for the witch who came to see me yesterday. Now it's all wasted!'

'A spell!' cried his wife, in dismay. 'Good gracious, Baby has licked some of it! Will it do him any harm?'

'I shouldn't think so,' said the wizard. 'We must wait and see.'

Well, for a little while the wizard and his wife saw nothing wrong with their son. He grew well, and was soon twice as big as children of his age. Everyone said what a fine boy he was, and how strong he looked.

But as he grew older, he shot up so tall, and became so broad, that folk began to wonder.

'He's much too tall for his age,' said one to another. 'There must be a spell on him. Why, he's only five years old, and yet he's much taller than his father, Deep-Eyes.'

Deep-Eyes soon knew what had happened. The spell he had made to make the witch's apple-trees grow bigger and stronger was acting on his little boy, and making him grow huge. Soon the wizard and his wife were quite afraid of Ho-Ho, for if they would not allow him to do something he wanted to do, he would smack them hard, and he was so strong and big that he made them howl with pain.

So very soon he was allowed to do just as he liked, and everyone in the town tried to please him for fear he should smack them with his enormous hand. This was very bad for Ho-Ho, and he grew up selfish and unkind.

When he was twenty years old he was simply enormous. He reached up to the clouds and his feet were as big as a large field. His voice was louder than

thunder, and he ate more food than a hundred men could eat at each meal.

Nobody knew what to do with him. The whole town had to find food for him, and if by chance he did not have enough to eat, he would stamp his great feet till houses fell to pieces and everyone shook and shivered in fear.

At last he stopped growing, but he was easily the biggest giant in the world, and the most selfish. Nobody knew what to do with Ho-Ho, for he would not work. He told everyone they must work for him, or he would smash the town to bits.

One winter it was very cold indeed, and Ho-Ho commanded the towns-people to build him a great castle. But though they tried their best they could not build one that reached to the top of the giant's head. So they decided that he would be better off in a deep cave under the earth.

'You will be warm there, Ho-Ho,' they said. 'The frost will not reach you, and you will be sheltered from the wind. There is not enough stone in the kingdom to build a castle big enough for you, so you must be content with a cave. We will do our best to make it very comfortable.'

At first Ho-Ho wouldn't listen, and demanded his castle – but soon he began to think that he might indeed be very cosy in a deep cave, and he told the little people to find one for him.

They did not trouble to find one. They asked Deep-Eyes the wizard to make one for them, and he brewed a very strong magic, said seven strange words, and emptied the magic on to the ground. Lo and behold, a cave opened beneath his feet large enough to hold a dozen giants in comfort.

'Ho-Ho should be very comfortable in such a large cave,' said the people. The giant had his bed put there, a chair, and a table, and soon made himself cosy.

'If only we could keep him there for always!' sighed the people. 'But in the spring he is sure to come out again, trample on our houses, and frighten everyone till they shiver and shake.'

'Couldn't we manage to tie him up?' asked Twinkles, a small pixie.

'Pooh!' said the chief man of the town, 'What an idea! Who do you suppose is going to tie Ho-Ho up, I should like to know!'

'I might be able to,' said Twinkles. 'I could think of a plan, I'm sure.'

Everyone laughed loudly at him, and he went away rather red in the face. He packed his bag and caught the train to Fiddle-Dee, the village where a great blacksmith lived. Twinkles made his way to his house, and found the clever smith hard at work.

'Could you make me a steel chain so strong that it couldn't be broken by anyone in the world?' he asked.

'Easily!' laughed the smith. 'What will you pay me for it?'

'Well, I haven't any money at present,' said Twinkles, 'but if you really *can* make me a chain that no one can break, I shall be rich, and will pay you what you please.'

The smith agreed, and at once set to

work. For four weeks he laboured hard,
and at the end of that time he showed
Twinkles a steel chain so strong and
heavy that the little pixie could not
move even one link of it.

'That will never break!' said he
smith, proudly. 'You will have to hire
fifty horses to carry it for you.'

So Twinkles got fifty horses, and they dragged the great chain behind them to the town. Everyone came out to see it, and Twinkles explained that he had brought it to bind Ho-Ho with, so that he would never be able to get out of his cave.

'We will pretend to Ho-Ho that it is all a game,' said Twinkles. 'Come along to his cave and we shall all see what happens.'

So everyone trooped off to the cave where the giant lived.

'Ho-Ho!' cried Twinkles, peering down. 'Are you as strong as you were? There are some who say that your strength is failing!'

Ho-Ho growled angrily.

'Prove it!' he said, in a rage. 'I am stronger than any other giant in the world.'

'Well, here is a chain that surely even *you* cannot break!' said Twinkles, and he bade the horses gallop near.

Ho-Ho took one look at it and snorted in scorn.

'You may bind me as tightly as you please with a toy chain like that!' he said. 'I will snap it in a moment!'

This was just what Twinkles wanted. He called the strongest men of the town to him and very soon they were binding the giant tightly with the chain, and made one end fast to a great rock.

'Ha! You are bound now!' cried Twinkles, in delight. 'You cannot get free, Ho-Ho!'

But the giant only smiled. He stretched himself and pulled on the great chain. Snap, snap, snap! It broke in twenty places, and Ho-Ho was free once more!

Then all the people had to pretend to be full of wonder and delight, for they were afraid to let Ho-Ho know that they really *had* wanted to bind him fast. He smiled and laughed, thinking that they were all glad at his strength.

'Bring a bigger chain still!' he said. 'I'll show you what I can do! Why, I could break a chain twenty times stronger than that!'

'Oh, no, you couldn't!' cried everyone. 'You really couldn't, Ho-Ho!'

'Try me and see!' said the giant.

So off went Twinkles to the smith again, and told him what had happened.

'Make a chain twenty times as strong,' he begged him. 'Surely the

giant cannot break that!'

'I am surprised he could break the other,' said the smith, marvelling. 'Well, I will make this new chain for you, Twinkles, but I cannot make it alone. I must get twelve other smiths to help me.'

So he sent for twelve brothers of his, all famous smiths, and the thirteen set to work to make a chain stronger than had ever been seen in the world before. In three weeks it was finished, for the smiths worked all through the night as well as by day. It took a thousand great horses to drag it along, and everyone ran by the panting beasts and cheered them on.

When Ho-Ho saw the enormous chain he looked rather solemn.

'Ha, ha!' said Twinkles, seeing him look doubtfully at the chain. 'This is twenty times as strong, and you said you could easily break it! But now that you see it, you are afraid, Ho-Ho! Fancy

a great giant like you, the biggest in the world, being afraid! Well, well, we will not let you try to break it we will take it back from where we brought it.'

But Ho-Ho did not like being laughed at. He took another look at the chain, and then looked at his great arms.

'You may bind me!' he said in his thunderous voice. 'I am not afraid! You will see how easily I can snap your silly little chain in two!'

So a hundred strong men bound him, and made one end of the chain fast to the rock. Then everyone stood back to see what would happen. Ho-Ho took a deep breath, and then tugged hard at the chain. It held! He tugged again. Alas! It flew apart in six different places, and the giant was free!

Once again the people had to pretend to marvel at him, and to be glad that he had broken their chain. Ho-Ho smiled with pleasure, for he loved people to admire him. But he made up his mind not to be bound again, in case one day he could *not* get free.

'I am tired of this chain game,' he said. 'I will not be bound any more!'

Then everyone knew that it was no use to try to bind the giant, and very sadly they went away. But still Twinkles did not give up hope.

If thirteen strong smiths cannot help me, maybe one clever dwarf can get me what I want! he thought. So he packed his bag again and took the train that ran deep underground to the caverns of the mountain dwarfs. Soon he came to where Peer-About, one of the very cleverest of the dwarfs, had his home.

Peer-About had so much knowledge inside his head, that it had grown very big, whilst his arms and legs had remained small; so he was a strange-looking little person but kind-hearted and always willing to help anyone.

Twinkles told him all about Ho-Ho, and how he had broken the two chains.

'I suppose you can't help me?' he asked.

'I think I can,' said Peer-About, after he had thought for a moment. 'Stay here for a week, and I will give you something that no giant, were he as big as the world itself, could break!'

So for a week Twinkles stayed with Peer-About in his little underground cave, and watched him work. The dwarf took the oddest things and mixed them all in a pot together. He took the footfall of six tigers, a little of the arch of a rainbow, some water from a bottomless pool, and the roots of a high mountain. Many other things he took, too, that Twinkles did not know, and carefully he stirred them all up together, chanting such strange words as he did so that Twinkles felt the hair standing up on his head with fright.

When the mixture was ready the dwarf put his hands into it and then

drew them out again. The stuff clung to them like wet toffee, and the little dwarf wound it neatly round a pointed stick. It looked like glistening silver thread, no thicker than sewing-cotton on a reel. Peer-About wound it steadily round his stick, and at last there was nothing left in the bowl.

'Now I must put it out into the moonlight for one night,' he said, 'and it will be ready.'

'But, Peer-About, do you really think it will be strong enough?' asked Twinkles. 'Why, it looks so slender I feel I could snap it myself!'

The dwarf smiled and said nothing. All that night the stick of silver thread lay out in the moonlight, and in the morning Peer-About made it into a small, gleaming ball of thread, and gave it to Twinkles.

'No one in the world can break that,' he said. 'Not even I, who made it, can snap it in two!'

Twinkles thanked the dwarf, and set off back to his own land. When he arrived there he showed his friends what he had been to fetch and they all laughed at him. They unwound the thread and pulled it – but no matter how they tugged and twisted they could not break it.

'But surely Ho-Ho will be able to snap it easily!' said everyone. 'It is so slender and so thin. And how are we going to bind him with it? He said he would not be bound any more.'

'I have an idea,' said Twinkles. 'It is spring-time now and Ho-Ho will expect to leave his cave and come out into the sunshine again. We will bind daisies all

along the thread as if it were a daisy-chain and take it to him, pretending that we wish to deck him and lead him out into the sun. Then we will bind him tightly with it, and he will not be able to move!'

'Well, we will try,' said the little people, doubtfully. 'But we think that Ho-Ho will easily snap such a frail thread.'

Then everyone worked hard and picked hundreds of starry daisies, tying them prettily along the silver thread, so that it looked for all the world like a mile-long daisy-chain. When it was finished they went dancing and singing to the cave where Ho-Ho dwelt, as if they were full of joy at the spring-time.

Ho-Ho looked up in surprise.

'We have come to fetch you out into the sunshine, Ho-Ho,' said Twinkles. 'And see! We have made up a lovely daisy-chain! Will you have it round you?'

Ho-Ho put out his hand and felt the daisy-chain, wondering if there was a strong chain hidden among the flowers. But when he felt the slender silver thread he smiled, for that was nothing, he thought.

He allowed Twinkles to wind the daisy-chain round and round him, and then the pixie deftly tied one end to the great rock inside the cave, making it fast.

'Now come, Ho-Ho,' he said, skipping nimbly out of the cave. 'Come out into the sunshine, decked with daisies!'

Ho-Ho stood up and tried to move forward, but the silver thread held him to the rock. He tugged lightly, thinking that the daisy-chain had become entangled in something, but still he was held fast. In a temper he pulled hard, but it was of no use – he could not get away.

Then Ho-Ho knew that he had been tricked, and he roared so loudly that chimney-pots shivered on their roofs and nearly fell off. All the little folk fled away in a panic, stuffing their fingers into their ears. Ho-Ho tugged at the thread again and again, amazed that such a slender thing should hold him so tightly. The daisies fell off one by one, and the giant twisted the thread round his great fingers.

But try as he would he could not snap it. It was far stronger than either of the chains. It slid through his fingers, and he could get no grip on it.

Then he knew he was caught and he roared aloud again in rage. He stamped his enormous feet and the earth shook.

He banged on the cave walls with his fists, and the roof become so shaken that it dropped huge stones on to Ho-Ho's head, and made him angrier still.

All that day and all the night the giant roared and raged, whilst the people of the town crouched in their houses, wondering what would happen to them if the silver thread snapped in two. Only Twinkles was unafraid, for he knew what things it was made of.

Next day he went to the giant's cave and peered down into it.

'Listen to me, Ho-Ho,' he said sternly. 'You are bound here for ever, but it is your own fault, for you are an unkind and selfish giant, of no use to anyone. Therefore you are made a prisoner. If you are quiet and peaceful, we will feed you each day, but if you roar and rage, you will starve.'

Ho-Ho listened and knew that he was defeated. He lay down quietly, and begged Twinkles to send him some food, promising to be good if only he might have something to eat.

Off went Twinkles, and soon all the people in the town had heard the great news – the biggest giant in the world was imprisoned and bound, and could never get away. How they cheered Twinkles and clapped him on the back!

They gave him one hundred sacks of gold, and he at once paid the thirteen smiths who had tried so hard to make chains strong enough for Ho-Ho.

Then with the rest of the money he bought a fine little cottage, married a pretty little wife, and settled down happily ever after.

As for Ho-Ho, he is usually quiet enough – but sometimes, when the little people bring him food he doesn't like, he gets into one of his old rages. Then he roars and bellows, stamps and kicks, and somewhere in the world there is an earthquake!

But you needn't be afraid that Ho-Ho will ever escape – the little silver thread that Peer-About the dwarf made will hold him fast until the end of the world!

Blackberry Pie

Andrew was cross. Just as he had planned to go blackberrying with the other children, Mother had called him to go on an errand for her!

'Oh, Mother, I wanted to go and pick some blackberries with Peter and Charlotte!' he grumbled. 'I did want you to make me a blackberry pie tomorrow! It's too bad!'

'I'm sorry, Andrew, but I promised Mrs Jones she should have these books back today,' said Mother, putting four books into a basket for Andrew to carry. 'Now don't sulk – you'll grow up ugly if you do!'

Andrew said no more. He was fond of

his mother, and he wasn't really a sulky boy. So he smiled at her and ran off – but inside he was very disappointed. It would have been so lovely to go blackberrying. There wouldn't be another chance till the next Saturday now, and it might be wet then. Bother, bother, bother!

He met Peter and Charlotte with their little baskets. 'Aren't you coming?' they shouted.

'I can't,' said Andrew. 'I've got to go into the town to take these books to Mrs Jones.'

'Bad luck,' said Peter, and he and Charlotte went on their way to the fields. Andrew began to whistle. He always found that it was a very good thing to do when he felt cross. You can't feel cross if you are whistling!

He came to Mrs Jones' house. She was at home and very glad to have the books. 'It's nice of you to bring them, Andrew,' she said. 'You might have been out in the fields with the others today, and then I wouldn't have got my books!'

'Well, I *was* going blackberrying, but Mother just called me before I went,' said Andrew.

'So you couldn't go blackberrying?' said Mrs Jones. 'What a pity! But listen, Andrew – at the bottom of my garden a great bramble grows over the fence. I don't like blackberries, so I haven't even looked to see if there are any growing there this year. Would you like to go and see? If there are any you can pick them all!'

'Oh, thank you!' said Andrew, pleased. He went down the garden and came to the bottom – and, sure enough, all over the fence there grew an enormous bramble! And on it were hundreds and hundreds of the biggest, ripest blackberries that Andrew had ever seen! Not one had been picked, and they grew there in the sunshine, full of ripe sweetness.

'Goodness gracious!' said Andrew, astonished and delighted. 'Look at those! My goodness, I'm lucky!' He began to pick them. He ate a great many. They were the sweetest he had ever tasted! More and more he picked, and more and more. His basket began to get full. His hands were wet and sticky. His mouth was purple. He was very happy indeed!

When his basket was full he went to show it to Mrs Jones. 'Splendid!' she said. 'I'm so glad they will not be wasted. Ask your mother to make you a blackberry pie with them. You deserve them.'

On his way home Andrew met Peter and Charlotte, and they were surprised to see his lovely big basketful. They had hardly any, for other children had been to the fields that day and picked all the ripe berries.

'Well, have some of mine!' said Andrew, and he emptied some into their baskets. They *were* pleased! Then home he went – and his mother cried out in astonishment.

'You *have* been blackberrying after all!' How she smiled when she heard Andrew's story – and now a big blackberry tart is baking in her oven. I'd *love* to have a slice, wouldn't you?

The Singing Shell

Once upon a time there was a brownie who lived underneath a mountain, far inland. He had never been further than his mountain. He had been to the bottom and seen the river that wound its way along the green valley. He had been to the top and shivered in the snow that always capped the tall mountain.

Every time he had climbed to the top there had been clouds there – great white mists that swirled around him so that he could see no further than a few metres before him. But one fine summer's day there were no clouds at all.

The brownie climbed to the top, panting and puffing, for the way was long and steep. He was surprised to see no white mists, but he did not look round until he reached the very top.

And then what a sight he saw! At his feet the whole countryside lay smiling in the sun! Green meadows, yellow fields of corn, dark woods, blue hills in the distance, silver rivers winding slowly along. And beyond, far beyond, lay something else, something that shone and glittered.

'What's that?' said the brownie to the eagle who lived on the mountain-top. The eagle gazed at the shining thing and said:

'That is the sea, the great, wide, singing sea. You should visit it, brownie, and make friends with the mermaids and mermen. They are your cousins.'

So the brownie packed his bag and went down the mountain. He followed green valley after green valley and at last he came to the sea.

There were hundreds of children there, paddling, bathing and digging. The brownie hid behind a rock and watched them. Then he slipped into a pool and went to seek his sea cousins.

He spent the whole summer by the sea, playing with the mermaids and mermen. He made himself a slippery suit of seaweed and a necklace of shells. Once he even played with some children, and they didn't guess he was a brownie. He had a perfectly lovely time, and grew as brown as his name!

But the longest of holidays comes to an end. The day came when the brownie had to say goodbye to his new friends and go back to his mountain-home. He was sad, and he wept tears into a pool.

'I wish I could take the sea with me!' he said. 'I wish I could take the lovely, lovely sound of the endless waves breaking and sighing on the sands! If only I could!'

'We'll give you the sound of the sea for a parting present,' said a mermaid,

and she picked up a big curly shell. She let a little wave break into it, and then she emptied out the salt water and gave the shell to the brownie. 'Put it to your ear,' she said. 'Whenever you long for the sea, listen to your shell. You will hear it there!'

And sure enough, when the brownie held the big shell to his ear, he heard the sighing of the waves inside! How delighted he was! 'Sh-sh!' sang the shell, 'Sh-sh, sh-sh-sh!'

He took it home with him and put it on his mantelpiece in his cave beneath the mountain. Every time he longed for the sea he put the shell to his ear and heard the lovely sound of the waves.

And the strange thing is that ever since that day all big shells have the sound of the sea inside them – a lovely magical sound that anyone can hear.

The Frightened Teddy-Bear

Once upon a time Jane took her teddy-bear out shopping, and carried him all the way, because he was not very big.

On the way home the little girl's shoe came undone, and she popped the bear down on a nearby step and did it up. But, oh dear me, when she stood up and went on her way again, she quite forgot to take her little bear!

There he sat on the doorstep of a strange house, lost and alone. He saw Jane running away in the distance, and watched for her to turn back and fetch him – but she didn't. She had remembered that there was chocolate pudding for dinner, and was running home as fast as she could.

Then a large sandy cat came along and looked at the bear.

'What are you doing here?' asked the cat. 'That is my doorstep you are sitting on. How dare you?'

'I'm very sorry,' said the little bear, getting up in a hurry. 'I really didn't know. My owner left me here.'

'Well, just remove yourself,' said the cat, sitting down and curling its big tail round its body. 'I've no use for bears.'

The sandy cat put out its paw and gave the Teddy a sharp push. He fell down the step on to his nose, and then, afraid that the cat would scratch him, he jumped to his feet and hurried down the road.

Two boys and a girl suddenly saw him and stopped in surprise.

'Ooh, look!' said the girl. 'A bear walking all by himself.'

'Let's catch him!' cried the boys, and they all set off after the bear in a hurry. He was very frightened and began to run. The children tore after him, and down the street they all sped, the little bear a good way ahead.

He puffed and panted, and felt sure that they would soon catch him. He came to the corner of the road and ran round it. Just near-by was a baker's cart, the back door of which was open, showing all the loaves there. The little bear suddenly gave a jump and landed among the loaves. Then he hid there, crouching behind a big currant loaf.

The three children turned the corner, and were astonished to see that the bear had vanished.

'Where's he gone?' they said, standing so close to the baker's cart that the little bear was afraid they would see him.

'Perhaps he's run into one of the gardens,' said the little girl. 'Let's look into each one and see.'

So down the street they went, peeping into each garden. Soon they were out of sight and the bear heaved a big sigh.

He was just going to scramble out of the cart when the baker came for his loaves, and put his hand in to get the big currant loaf. He saw the little bear

and cried out in surprise.

'Oh, my!' he said. 'Whatever's this?'

The bear leapt out of the van, and then took to his heels and ran. The baker made a grab at him and missed. Then, full of surprise at the sight of a running teddy-bear, he put down his basket and chased him.

The bear ran on and on, hearing the baker just behind him. Then suddenly the man slipped and fell, and by the time he had picked himself up again the little bear had gone.

He had run down a little pathway and come to a field of buttercups. He flung himself down on the grass and panted, for he was really out of breath.

'Whatever shall I do?' he wondered. 'I am quite lost. Oh dear, I do feel miserable.'

Two large tears came into his boot-button eyes and trickled down his furry brown nose – but, dear me, he hadn't time even to cry, for at that moment up came a large black dog, and sniffed hard at the frightened bear.

Teddy jumped to his feet in dismay. What a dreadful creature! Would it eat him? He saw what large strong teeth the dog had, and once more the little bear began to run.

He ran through the golden butter-cups, and the dog ran after him. But this time the little bear could not run very fast, for he was tired. He looked back and saw that the dog would soon catch him up.

'Oh, what shall I do?' he groaned. 'I shall certainly be eaten if I am caught!'

Now just at that moment the bear saw an old kite lying on the grass. It had once belonged to a little boy who had flown it on a very windy day. The wind had broken the string and the kite had flown off by itself, coming to rest in the field, where it had lain for many days.

'Oh, kite!' cried the little bear, running up to it, 'please, please help me! Take me away from this horrid big dog!'

The bear held on to the tail of the kite, which suddenly rose in the air, taking its unusual little passenger with it. The dog stopped in amazement, and then tried to jump up and snap at the bear – but the kite was now too high, and the dog was soon left behind.

The bear hung on to the tail for all he was worth, and the kite sailed steadily through the air.

'I shall have to come down in a minute,' said the kite. 'The wind is dropping, and I can't fly without wind, you know.'

The wind dropped, and the kite dropped too. Down it went and down, and soon it lay quietly on the grass in someone's garden. A little girl came running from the house to see what it was – and goodness, wasn't the teddy-bear astonished to see her!

It was Jane, his little owner, who

had left him behind by mistake!

'Oh, the kite has brought my teddy back to me!' cried Jane, picking him up and hugging him. 'Oh, you dear little bear! I thought I had lost you for ever, for when I went back to look for you, you were gone! Oh, how lovely to see you again! And how kind of the kite to bring you! It's a dirty old thing, but it shall live in the nursery, because I'm so glad it brought you back again!'

So the kite went upstairs with the teddy-bear, who was delighted to be safe home once more. All his friends were pleased to see him again, and weren't they surprised to hear the tale of his adventures!

As for the kite, he was quite a hero, and he and the teddy-bear were fast friends forever.

The Old Boot

There was once an old boot. It lay in a ditch, burst open at the toes, worn down at the heel and with its laces missing. Once it had been a very grand boot – so grand that it had been worn by a prince. Think of that! It had been proud then, with a servant to polish it up every day and to make it shine brilliantly. Its brother boot lived with it, and they talked together all day long, very happily.

Then the prince bought some new boots, and gave his old ones to his servant. The man was proud to have such grand boots and wore them every Sunday – but when they wanted mending he couldn't be bothered with them, and he told his wife to give them away at the door next time a pedlar came round with some plants. So the boots were given to a ragged old pedlar, and he gave the servant's wife a fine fern for them.

They did not fit the pedlar very well, especially one of them, for his right foot was much bigger than his left. They were never cleaned now, and never mended. They grew old and wrinkled, and one of them burst at the toes. The pedlar grumbled bitterly at the boots, and one day, when he found an old shoe by the roadside, he flung off one of the boots, put on the shoe instead, and threw the old boot into the ditch. Then, limping, he went off down the road, wearing one boot and one shoe.

Then the old boot in the ditch was lonely, for it no longer had its brother boot to talk with. Spiders ran over it. A beetle went inside it. The rain soaked it

through and through, and some grass seeds took root inside and grew there. The boot was sad and ashamed to think what it had come to. No one cared about it now, lost and forgotten in a wayside ditch.

Then one day in spring a red-breasted robin flew down to the ditch and turned over some dead leaves there. He saw the old boot and perched on the side, peering this way and that. Then he uttered a little trill and called his wife to him.

"See! what a wonderful place for a nest! You know how we robins love to build in something that has belonged to man, our friend. Well, here is a splendid boot, just right for a nest! What a piece of luck!'

Then, to the great delight of the old boot, the robins built their nest there. How carefully they built it of grass-roots, fibres, moss and leaves! The boot marvelled at the way they used their beaks to weave such a cosy home. It liked to feel their tiny feet perching here and there, and loved to listen to their creamy voices when they sang.

Four speckled eggs were laid in the old boot. How proud it was! And how much prouder when the eggs hatched out into tiny birds, which were soon

The Old Boot

covered with softest down and feathers. It listened contentedly to their chatter, and was excited when they first tried their tiny wings.

'Thank you, old boot!' sang the robins, when their youngsters had all flown. 'You kept our family safe!'

The boot was lonely when the robins were gone – but an adventure was still to come to it. For one day two children found it, with the old robins' nest still inside.

'A find, a find!' they cried. 'Let's take it to school, and put it in the museum there! Everyone will love to see it!'

They did, and now the old boot has the place of honour in the school museum and is as happy as can be.

The Rabbit That Didn't Grow Up

Loppy was a little sandy rabbit who lived with all his brothers and sisters in a cosy burrow. Loppy had one brown ear and one black one, and a little bobtail that was snow-white underneath.

At first Loppy was just like his brothers and sisters, but after a little while his mother noticed that he didn't seem to grow.

'Isn't it strange?' she said to Loppy's father. 'All the other children have grown fat and big, but Loppy is still a baby rabbit.'

When his brothers and sisters grew up and left home, Loppy was still small and babyish. He didn't grow up at all, and all day long he wanted to play. His mother couldn't understand him, and grew quite cross.

'You are too old to play silly games now, Loppy,' she said. 'Why, look at all your brothers and sisters! They have cosy burrows of their own and have married and got dear little baby rabbits. *You* are just as much a baby as ever.'

Loppy was unhappy. He didn't know why he hadn't grown up, and he couldn't help it. He tried to stop playing, but he soon forgot and started to have a game of chase-my-tail as soon as he got outside the burrow.

After a little while the grown-ups took no notice of him. He hadn't grown up, so he must just stay a baby rabbit, that was all. Loppy didn't mind that, but when the young rabbits wouldn't let him play with them, he was very sad.

'Why can't I play with you?' he said. 'I like games as much as you do.'

'Yes, but you are much, much older than we are,' said the young rabbits scornfully. 'It is silly of you to want to play games with us when you aren't young. You ought to go about with the grown-up rabbits.'

ey don't want me,' said Loppy, . 'Nobody wants me. I do wish I could grow up, but I can't.'

He was so unhappy that he made up his mind to go away and leave his home. So one day he set off, and after he had run for many miles he came to a pretty garden. He peeped in and saw a little girl sitting there playing at tea-parties. She had sat her dolls all round her in a ring, together with a teddy-bear and a toy rabbit, a monkey, and she was pretending to give them tea.

'Ooh, what a lovely game,' said Loppy. 'I wish I could play that too. And look how she's cuddling that teddy-bear! *I* should like to be cuddled like that.'

Just then the little girl's mother called her and she ran indoors, leaving all her toys where they were. Loppy ran up to them and sat himself down in the ring.

'I want to play this game too,' he said.

'But you can't!' said the biggest doll. 'You're not a toy. It's only toys that can

play like this.'

'Can't a live rabbit play too?' asked Loppy.

'Oh no,' said the teddy. 'Of course not.'

'Do you play games every single day and never stop?' asked Loppy. 'Do you still go on playing when you're grown up?'

'Toys never grow up,' said the monkey. 'Didn't you know *that*? So we play games all our day long and never get tired of them.'

'Ooh!' said Loppy, with a sigh. 'I wish I was a toy then. I'm a rabbit that has never grown up and I do wish I knew how to change into a toy bunny.'

'I never heard of a live animal wanting to change into a toy before!' said the biggest doll. 'I've heard of plenty of toys that wanted to come alive, but it seems funny to want to be a toy if you're something *real*.'

'If you go to Toyland, perhaps they'll change you into a toy,' said the teddy. 'They can do all sorts of wonderful things there.'

'Oh, do tell me the way!' begged Loppy. So the toys told him, and he set off at once. He travelled all that day and all the night, and early the next morning he arrived at the gates of Toyland.

'What do you want?' asked the gatekeeper, seeing a live rabbit there. 'You're not a toy.'

'No, but I want to be,' said Loppy.

'Well, *that's* a funny thing!' said the gatekeeper, and he let Loppy in. 'You'd better go to that castle high on the hill there, where Santa Claus lives. Maybe he can do something for you.'

So Loppy went to the castle and saw jolly old Santa Claus. He told him all his troubles, and what a dreadful thing it was to be a rabbit that never grew up, and Santa Claus listened, nodding his head.

'Well, if you become a toy, you will lose any chance you have of ever being grown-up,' he said, 'for toys never change, you know. Are you sure you will never get tired of being played with and of playing games all your life long?'

'Quite,' said Loppy.

'Well, sit on that little stool, and I will give you something to drink which will change you from a live rabbit into a toy one,' said Santa Claus. 'Then next Christmas-time I will put you in my sack and pop you into some child's stocking.'

So in great excitement Loppy sat down on the little stool. Santa Claus mixed him a strange-looking drink. It was blue with yellow specks floating in it, and Loppy felt as if he were drinking fire when it ran down his throat. No sooner had he drunk it than he felt very different, though he looked just the same as ever. He had become a toy rabbit!

When Christmas-time came, Santa

Claus stuffed Loppy into his sack with hundreds of other toys and set off on his rounds. He put Loppy into a little girl's stocking together with a doll and a teddy-bear and then went off to the next chimney.

'Oh!' cried the little girl next morning. 'What a lovely cuddlesome bunny! It looks just like a real one! Oh, how I shall love it! Dear little bunny, I do hope you will be happy in my nursery with all my other toys.'

Well, you can guess that Loppy was as happy as the day was long! Nobody jeered at him because he hadn't grown up, because none of the other toys could grow up either. He played games all day long, and at night the little girl took him to bed with her and cuddled him till the morning.

And if any of your friends has a toy rabbit with one ear brown and the other ear black, take a good look at him, because he may be Loppy, the rabbit who never grew up!

Upadee and the Dragon

Upadee was a wicked little tease. He was a pixie who lived by the old pond in the wood, and he teased everything and everybody he met. He teased the sticklebacks in the pond, the chaffinches that sipped water from it, the swallows that flew above it, and the sandy rabbits that played round about.

But most of all he teased the big brown grub in the pond. Upadee used to swim there every day, and loved to dive under the water and talk to the creatures below. He knew the beetles well, and often played with the young frogs that had been tadpoles that year – but he never had a good word to say to the ugly brown grub.

It was a long, jointed creature with strange pincers that caught smaller insects as they came swimming by. It had six legs, and liked to creep along in the mud at the bottom of the pond. Upadee the pixie jeered at the strange grub.

'Ugly creature!' he called, swimming down to the mud where the grub was hiding. 'Look at your long jointed body, like an old-fashioned dragon! No wonder you hide yourself in the mud! I would, too, if I were as ugly as you!'

'I can't help being ugly,' said the grub dolefully.

'You are growing bigger and uglier every day!' cried Upadee, and brought a shoal of little sticklebacks to laugh at the grub. 'You have been here two years now, you horrid water-dragon, and it's a pity you don't find another home, for who wants to know a hideous creature like you?'

The grub said nothing. It didn't like being called a dragon, for it sounded a horrid name. It didn't like being jeered at, and it wished it were beautiful like the shining sticklebacks or the little green frogs with their gleaming eyes.

One sunny day a brownie riding a butterfly came to see Upadee, and asked him to come for a ride. But all the bumble-bees were too busy to take him, and each butterfly was already ridden by one of the little folk in the wood.

'Well, well!' said the brownie, peering into the pond, *'I'll* get you a steed, Upadee!'

He tapped the water with his wand. Below, in the mud, lay the brown grub. Suddenly a curious feeling came over him. He felt as if he *must* climb up a stalk, and go right out of the water, a thing he had never done before! So up he went. And when he was clinging to the stalk above the water, the hot sunshine stinging him, a strange thing happened! His skin split all the way down his back! Upadee the pixie watched in astonishment.

'Look at the ugly old dragon-grub!'

he shouted scornfully. 'Whatever does he think he's doing?'

The grub certainly didn't know – he only felt that he *must* wriggle out of his skin somehow or other. So he struggled out – and when he was out, marvel of marvels, he was quite a different creature! He had four gleaming wings and a bright blue body, slender as a bodkin. His eyes were large and absolutely wonderful.

'There's your steed!' said the brownie, laughing at Upadee's astonished face. 'Ride him! He's a dragonfly.'

'*Ride* me!' cried the dragonfly in scorn. 'Upadee shall *not* ride me! He made me miserable when I was an ugly grub, and I am not going to make him happy now I am a beautiful dragonfly! Horrid little tease!'

And with that the dragonfly rose up into the air, flicked Upadee with his gleaming wings, and flew off into the wood, happy, beautiful and free. As for Upadee, he went very red, ran home and vowed never in his life to tease any one again.

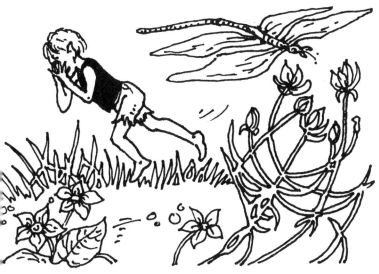

The Tale of Higgle and Hum

Once upon a time the King of Fairyland went to his magic cupboard and found that a thief had been there in the night.

'My goodness!' cried the king, in a great way. 'Robbers! Now what have they taken?'

He called the queen and together they went through all the things in the magic cupboard, and they found that three had been stolen.

'There's my magic lamp gone!' said the king in dismay. 'The one that lights up the whole of the wood when the moon doesn't shine for our dances.'

'And where are my magic scissors?' said the queen, with a groan. 'The pair that will cut through anything – iron, steel or stone!'

'And my fine walking stick,' said the king, sadly. 'I'm sorry that has been stolen, because I had only to say, "Up, stick, and at him!" and it would jump up and beat any rogue I met.'

'How shall we get our things back?' wondered the queen. 'And who has taken them?'

They soon found out who the thief was. It was a goblin called Groo, a cunning fellow who had long wanted these three things for himself.

'He is so clever that I am afraid we shall never have our magic things again,' said the queen, with a sigh. 'If we sent our soldiers against him, he would simply turn them all into an army of ants, and that would be dreadful.'

'Well, we'll send out a proclamation saying that if anyone can get back our magic things for us we will give him a sack of gold, a beautiful palace and a free invitation to all our dances and parties,' said the king.

So this was done, and soon all the elves, pixies, fairies, gnomes and brownies were talking excitedly of how the three things belonging to the king might be taken from Groo the goblin.

First an elf tried, and, oh dear me, he was turned into a frog, and it took the king a very long time to find the right spell that would change him back into his own shape again. Then two gnomes tried and they were turned into earwigs. They went to the king in a fright, and he had to pay a wise man twenty

pieces of gold to change them back again.

After that no one tried, for everyone was afraid. Then one day there came wandering into Fairyland two imps called Higgle and Hum. As soon as they heard of the king's message they looked at one another in delight.

'*We'll* get the things back!' they cried.

'Easier said than done!' said a listening brownie. 'You don't know how clever Groo the goblin is!'

154

Higgle and Hum said no more, but went off to a sunny hedgeside to talk about how they should get into Groo's house.

'We've been poor and ragged all our lives,' said Higgle, 'and we've never had a chance of being rich, or having nice shoes and clothes. Why, we haven't ever been to a party or a dance, because we were so raggedy! How fine it would be to have a sack of gold and live in a palace on a hill! And oh, think of going to every single party that the king and queen give! What a fine time we should have!'

'How shall we get the magic things, though?' asked Hum. 'Hadn't we better make a plan?'

They thought and thought, and at last decided that it wasn't a bit of good making a plan – they had just better see what they could do, and make plans as they went along.

That night they crept into the garden of Groo's house, and peered in through the kitchen window.

'Look!' whispered Higgle. 'There's the magic lamp on the dresser!'

'And there's the magic scissors in that work-basket!' said Hum. 'Where's the magic stick?'

'Standing in the corner yonder,' whispered Higgle. 'Oh! Oh! Oh!'

It was no wonder he cried out for someone had suddenly caught hold of him! It was Groo the goblin, and very soon he had Higgle in one hand and Hum in the other, both imps trembling with fright.

'Ho!' he said in a harsh voice. 'What are you doing peeping and prying into my kitchen, I should like to know? Don't you know that I can turn people into earwigs and frogs, if I want to?'

'Please, please don't do that!' said Higgle, in a fright. 'We were thinking what a nice warm kitchen you had, and wondering if you wanted any servants.'

'Well, my wife could do with two,' said Groo. 'I'll show you to her and see if she wants you. If she doesn't I'll have you cooked for my dinner.'

He took the shivering imps into his kitchen and showed them to his wife, who looked at them through her big glasses.

'Yes, they'll do nicely, dear,' she said to Groo. 'I'll have them for servants.'

'Well, if you get tired of them, let me know and I'll have them cooked for dinner,' said Groo. 'And mind, wife, don't you let them get away! They'll run if they have a chance, I'm sure of that. You keep them safely in the kitchen.'

'Very well, dear,' said Mrs Groo, and she turned to Higgle and Hum. 'Just draw some hot water from the tap and start to scrub the kitchen floor,' she said.

Groo the goblin went out of the room and banged the door. Higgle and Hum ran to the tap and got a pail of water. It was not very hot, and Higgle looked at the fire.

'Please, ma'am,' he said to Mrs Groo, 'the water isn't hot enough to scrub the floor properly. The fire has gone down and the water is cooling. Shall I stoke it up?'

'Oh dear, oh dear, there's no wood in the wood-box,' said the old dame in a flurry. 'I meant to have asked Groo this morning to chop some for me, and I quite forgot. What a temper he will be in when I ask him now, for he does hate to go out to the woodshed in the dark.'

'Well, ma'am, let *me* go,' said Higgle. 'I'm your servant, aren't I?'

'Of course!' said Mrs Groo. 'Well, out you go and chop me some wood – but don't be long.'

Higgle grinned at Hum and ran out. He didn't go to the woodshed, but hid outside the front gate. Soon Mrs Groo became impatient and wondered whatever Higgle was doing.

'Drat the imp!' she said. 'I suppose I must go and see if he's lost his way in the garden.'

'Ma'am let *me* go and find him!' said Hum, running over to her. 'Don't you go out in the darkness! Lend me that lamp on the dresser, and I'll soon find him!'

'Well, take it, and don't be long,' said Mrs Groo. She lighted the lamp and Hum took it. He ran out into the garden, puffed out the lamp, and made for the front gate. He found Higgle there, and together the two clever imps raced down the lane as fast as their legs would carry them, rejoicing that their trick had succeeded.

The king was delighted to get his

magic lamp, and he praised the two imps for being able to outwit the cunning old goblin.

'If only you can get the other things

I shall be overjoyed!' said the queen.

So the next night Higgle and Hum made their way quietly to Groo's house again, meaning to break in at the window when Groo had gone to bed, and take the scissors and magic stick. But the goblin was lying in wait for them, and pounced on the two scared imps just as they reached the front gate.

'Ha!' he said. 'Now I've got you again, and I can tell you, I won't let you go *this* time! I'll have you for my dinner tomorrow!'

He dragged the imps into the kitchen and shut them into the wood-box for the night. They could not get out, and they trembled there in fear, thinking that their end was very near this time. In the morning Mrs Groo took them out and looked at them.

'You are very naughty not to have come back the night I sent you to chop the wood,' she said. 'Now I've got to cook you for my husband's dinner, instead of having you for servants!'

The imps watched her stoke up the fire and trembled all the more. Then Higgle spoke.

'I suppose, ma'am, you've got plenty of killy-kolly leaves to cook with us?' he said. 'If imps are cooked without killy-kolly leaves, they will poison whoever eats them.'

'My goodness!' said Mrs Groo in fright. 'No, I didn't know that! Well, I've plenty of killy-kollies in my garden. I'd better go and pick some.'

'Let *me* pick them for you,' said Higgle. 'You've plenty to do in preparing the dinner, I'm sure.'

'All right, you may go and pick them,' said Mrs Groo, giving him a plate. 'But see that you keep in sight of the window, for if you run off again, Mr Groo will be very angry.'

Higgle took the plate, grinned at Hum and ran out into the garden to the killy-kolly bed. He began to pick some of the leaves, and he pretended that they were very hard indeed to pull from the stems. Mrs Groo became impatient, and called out of the window to him.

'Hurry up, now, hurry up! I'm waiting for that dish of leaves. What a time you take picking them!'

'Please, ma'am, they're very hard to pick,' said Higgle, standing up in the killy-kolly bed. 'Could you send Hum out with a pair of strong scissors? Then I could cut the leaves off easily, and bring them in to you at once.'

Mrs Groo went to her work-basket and took out the pair of magic scissors there. She gave them to Hum and bade him take them to Higgle, and then come back to help her peel some potatoes. Hum ran off, and as soon as Higgle saw him coming he ran to the front

gate, and down the lane the two imps tore as fast as they could.

How glad they were to be free, and to have the magic scissors! They took them to the king and he was delighted.

'You're a very clever pair!' he said. 'Now if only you can get me my magic stick, I shall be very happy.'

The two imps didn't dare to go near Groo's house at once, for they knew he would be on the watch for them. But at last, after ten days had gone by, Higgle and Hum went once more to the goblin's house, and this time they crept in at the back door.

But oh dear me, who should spy them but old Mrs Groo, and she caught them and dragged them into her kitchen.

'So it's you again!' she said. 'Well, you ran away last time with the magic scissors, and the time before with the magic lamp – but this time you *won't* get away! Mr Groo beat me for letting you go, but he will be pleased with me now for catching you!'

'Where *is* Groo?' asked Higgle, looking round.

'He's gone to see his friend, Mr Topple,' said Mrs Groo, 'but don't you fret! He won't be long, I can tell you, and I shouldn't be surprised if he has you for his supper as soon as he comes home.'

Higgle and Hum were frightened. They felt quite sure that they really would be eaten this time, and they tried in vain to think of some way of escape.

Mrs Groo sat down to her sewing, and for some time there was silence in the warm kitchen. Then the clock struck nine, and Mrs Groo looked up in surprise.

'Dear dear!' she said. 'How late Groo is! I do hope he hasn't got lost on this dark night.'

'Shall I go and look for him?' asked Higgle.

'No, that you won't!' said Mrs Groo, sharply.

'Well, ma'am, just let me go to the front door and peep out,' said Higgle. 'You can see I don't escape then, can't you, but as I have very sharp eyes, I can see a long way and could tell you if your husband is coming.'

'Very well,' said Mrs Groo, 'but mind – if you so much as put a foot over the doorstep, I'll drag you in and put you into that saucepan, Higgle.'

Higgle grinned at Hum and went to the door to open it. He stood on the doorstep and peered this way and that. Suddenly he gave a shout.

'Robbers! Thieves! he cried. 'Look, robbers, thieves! Where's a stick! Bring a stick to beat them with!'

Mrs Groo began to tremble. She picked up the magic stick that stood in the corner and gave it to Hum, who ran to Higgle with it.

Sure enough, someone was coming up the front path, and Mrs Groo felt certain it must be robbers. She began to scream.

'Up, stick, and at him!' shouted Higgle, and at once the stick leapt from his hand and flew at the person coming up the path. How it beat him and whipped him! And how he yelled and shouted.

'I'm no robber, I'm Groo the goblin! Call the stick off, call it off! I'm Groo the goblin, I tell you!'

But Higgle and Hum shouted, too, so loudly that Mrs Groo couldn't hear that it was her husband in the garden and not a robber. She hid herself in a corner, and didn't dream of calling the stick off.

Higgle and Hum ran to the back gate and halfway down the lane, grinning to think that the wicked goblin was having such a fine whipping.

Then Higgle put his hands to his mouth and shouted loudly:

'Stick, stick, come to me!'

The stick stopped beating Groo and flew to Higgle's hand. The two imps set off running as fast as they could and the goblin was so sore with his beating that he could not run after them, but could only stumble into his kitchen and sit down on a chair.

How delighted the king and queen were to see their magic stick safely back again!

'Surely you are the two cleverest

imps in the kingdom!' said the king. 'Well, you shall have your sack of gold, and your palace, and you may be sure you will receive a free invitation to every party and dance that the queen

gives. Thank you very much for all you have done.'

Then in delight the two imps took the gold and went to the palace that the king gave them. They bought themselves splendid new suits, took two pretty little wives, and lived happily in their glittering palace for ever after. They still go to every party in Fairyland, and though they must have been to thousands now, they haven't got tired of them yet!

As for Groo the goblin, he was so ashamed at being tricked by two imps that he packed up his things and he and Mrs Groo disappeared, nobody knew where – and nobody minded, either!

The Surprising Easter Egg

Anna was going to a party. She was all ready. She had on her new pink silk dress, a ribbon round her hair, her shoes in a bag, and a clean handkerchief in her pocket. She felt so excited, for she loved parties almost better than anything else.

'Now, it's time you started,' said Mother. 'Goodbye, Anna. Have a lovely time – and remember to say thank you very much to Mrs Jones when you leave.'

'I won't forget!' said Anna happily. She ran down the garden path and out into the lane. What fun it was to be going to a party! Little Louise Jones' birthday fell in Easter week this year, and it was going to be a lovely party, with an Easter egg for everyone to take home. Anna felt very happy.

She skipped down the lane past Mrs White's house. Anna always stopped and looked over the gate at Mrs White's, because she had two lovely Persian cats – blue-grey, with great orange eyes and long thick fur. Anna loved all animals – and wasn't it a pity, she had no pet of her own at all! No dog, no cat, not even a goldfish, lived at Anna's house. No one had thought of letting her have a pet. Anna's mother was not very fond of animals, so she didn't bother about them.

Anna looked over Mrs White's gate, hoping to see one of the lovely Persian cats somewhere in the garden. They loved Anna and always came running to her to be stroked. Anna knew that they had six little kittens just now –

and how she longed to see them! But Mrs White was rather a grand sort of lady, and Anna didn't like to ask her if she might go and see the kittens.

There were no cats in the garden at all, so Anna went on her way down the lane, thinking of the party, and wondering if there would be red or yellow jelly, and which she would choose. Halfway down the lane she passed an old tumbledown barn – and as she went by it she heard a noise that made her stop in surprise.

It was the mewing of cats! Now what could they be mewing for in the barn?

Anna stopped and looked round. She saw a curious sight! One of Mrs White's Persian cats was coming slowly along under the hedge – and in its mouth it carried one of its kittens! It was holding the kitten by the skin of its neck, as cats do. Anna was so surprised. She watched the cat slip under the hedge, make its way through the wet field, and disappear into the old barn.

The mewing still went on. Anna couldn't understand it. Mrs White's cat must have taken all her kittens into the barn, she thought. What a dreadful place to take them – so damp and cold and dirty! Poor little things!

Anna found a hole in the hedge and squeezed through it. She went to the barn and peeped in. It was dark and at first she could hardly see anything. Then she discovered where the kittens were.

The mother-cat had climbed up a plank, and had put all her six kittens, one by one, on a shelf in the barn. There was a hole in the barn wall just there, and the wind came in. The kittens were cold and frightened. One crawled about

the shelf – and then, to Anna's horror, it fell over the edge, bounced on the plank, and rolled to the ground!

It didn't seem to be hurt, but Anna was worried. Suppose they all fell off? Silly mother-cat, to put her kittens there!

Oh dear, I shall be late for the party, thought Anna, and I've got my best dress on. Whatever am I to do? I simply can't leave those kittens there.

She looked round for a ladder. There was an old one at the end of the barn. Anna dragged it across and put it up against the wall. She went up it and reached the shelf where the kittens were. There were five there – and one on the floor. The mother-cat was there too, and she purred when she saw Anna. Anna took hold of a kitten and carried it down the ladder. Then up she went again, and before long all six kittens were safely on the ground.

Then the little girl found an old basket, without a handle. She carefully put the kittens into it, and, with the mother-cat trotting beside her, she went out of the barn and back to Mrs White's house.

How delighted Mrs White was to have her kittens back again, safe and sound! She was hunting for them everywhere!

'A dog came into the house and frightened the mother-cat,' she told Anna. 'So I suppose she thought she had better take her kittens somewhere else. They would all have caught cold in that draughty barn. It *is* good of you to take so much trouble, Anna.'

'I love all animals,' said Anna, 'especially kittens. I'd love to have a pet of my own. Oh dear, look at my party dress! It's all dirty and I've torn it! I can't go to the party, I'm afraid!'

'Oh, I *am* sorry,' said Mrs White. 'Can't you go home and put another dress on?'

'I've only got my school dress besides this,' said Anna. 'It doesn't matter. I don't mind missing the party if I've rescued your kitten family! I do love them so much!'

So Anna missed the party, for she didn't want to go in her old school dress. She was very sad about it, and Mother was sorry for her. Mrs White had told Mother how kind Anna had been, so she understood all about it.

'Never mind, darling, you shall have an Easter egg,' said Mother, so Anna looked forward to that. She wondered if it would be a chocolate one. She did like chocolate very much.

There *was* a chocolate egg for her – and another egg, too – a most surprising Easter egg! Mother brought it into the dining-room with such a funny smile on her face. It was an *enormous* cardboard egg, red, yellow and blue – and it made a noise!

It did really! And what sort of a noise do you think it made? Guess!

It *mewed*! Anna gave a scream of excitement and split the egg in half – and out jumped the dearest, prettiest little Persian kitten you ever saw! It was one that Anna had rescued from the barn that week!

'Mrs White said that you were just the right person to have one of her kittens,' said Mother. 'Do you like your Easter egg, Anna?'

'Mother, it's the loveliest one in all the world!' cried Anna. 'Oh, I don't mind missing the party if I have a kitten of my own. I am *so* happy!'

Wasn't it a surprising Easter egg?